To: ....

From: ....

GROSSET & DUNLAP
An Imprint of Penguin Random House LLC, New York

Published in the United States of America in 2020 by Grosset & Dunlap,
an imprint of Penguin Random House LLC, New York. GROSSET & DUNLAP is a trademark
of Penguin Random House LLC. Manufactured in China.

Visit us online at www.penguinrandomhouse.com.

www.mrmen.com

The publisher does not have any control over and does not assume any
responsibility for author or third-party websites or their content.

ISBN 9780593094167   10 9 8 7 6 5 4 3 2 1

MY BROTHER

and me

by Roger Hargreaves

Grosset & Dunlap

My brother welcomes every day with
a smile on his face.

He is full of energy.
He doesn't walk down
the stairs,
he bounces
down
them!

My brother is so funny,
he even
makes
lions
laugh.

Life is never dull when he is there.

He makes
every day more
magical.

And he tells the best stories, but
I'm not always sure if they're true.

He is very brave
and makes impossible things look easy.

But he can get scared, just like me.

He is always surprising me with his tickles.

And he knows just how to cheer me up when I'm feeling sad.

My brother loves eating
and sometimes his
eyes are bigger
than his belly.

But his food doesn't always end up in his mouth!

My brother can be as messy as Mr. Messy.

And as mischievous

as Mr. Mischief.

My brother is so much fun to be around.

But he can be a bit grumpy when things don't go his way.

My brother doesn't always do what he's told.

And he sometimes goes
b^ump when he isn't careful.

My brother
loves animals,
particularly the
noisy, messy
kind.

He also loves books and would like to
be in his own one day—and now he is!

He really is one of a kind.

And he even sleeps in his own unique way.

He would love to swim in a sea of candy!

He is so cool,
and when we're together
the most amazing things happen.

My brother is the **greatest** brother ever.

MY BROTHER

My brother is most like **MR.** ....

I love it when my brother plays...

....with me.

My brother makes me laugh when ....

....

He is very silly because..

....

My brother gets into trouble when he ....

....

He is lots of fun and likes ....

Our favorite thing to do together is ....

One day he will be a famous ....

My brother is the greatest because ....

....

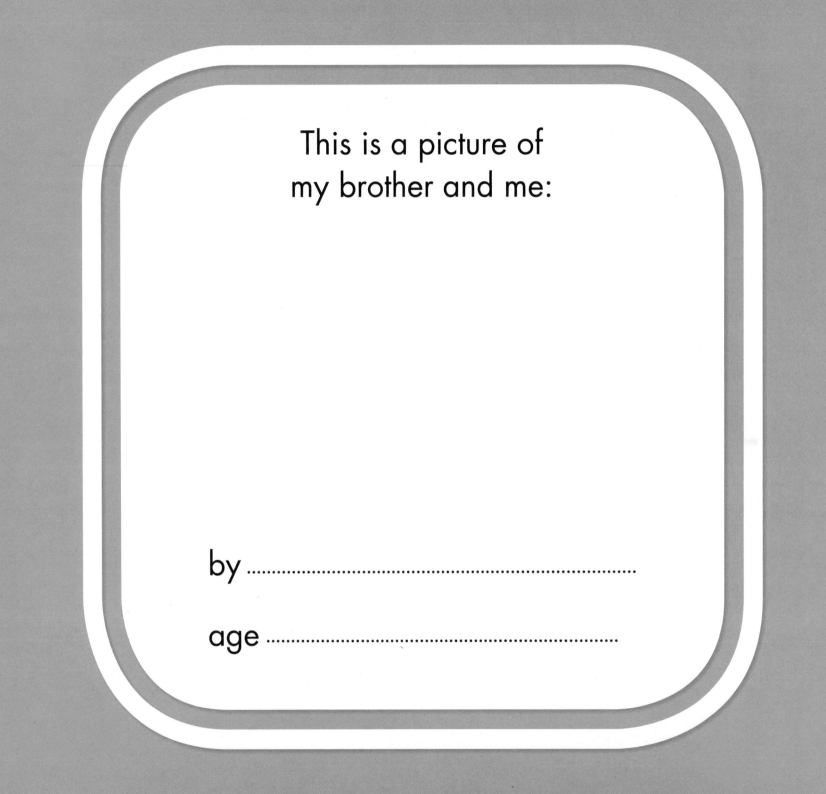

This is a picture of
my brother and me:

by ....

age ....